MW00977970

THERE WAS AN OLD MONSTER!

Sing along with this book!
To download your free copy of the song for
There Was An Old Monster, please go to
www.scholastic.com/oldmonster

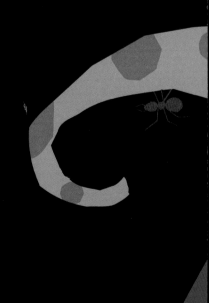

Rebecca, Adrian & Ed Emberley

There Was an Old Monster!

ORCHARD BOOKS
An Imprint of Scholastic Inc.
New York

All rights reserved. Published by Orchard Books, an imprint of Scholastic Inc., *Publishers since 1920.*
ORCHARD BOOKS and design are registered trademarks of Watts Publishing Group, Ltd., used under license.
SCHOLASTIC and associated logos are trademarks and/or registered trademarks of Scholastic Inc.

Library of Congress Cataloging-in-Publication Data:
Emberley, Rebecca.
There was an old monster / by Rebecca Emberley; illustrated by Rebecca Emberley and Ed Emberley;
music by Rebecca Emberley and Adrian Emberley.
p. cm.
Summary: In this variation on the traditional cumulative rhyme, a monster swallows ants, a lizard, a bat,
and other creatures to try to cure a stomachache that began when he swallowed a tick.

ISBN-13: 978-0-545-10145-5 (reinforced lib. bdg.)
ISBN-10: 0-545-10145-X (alk. paper)

1. Folk songs, English—Texts. [1. Folk songs. 2. Nonsense verses.]
I. Emberley, Ed, ill. II. Emberley, Adrian. III. Title.
PZ8.3.E517The 2007
782.42—dc22
LOC: 2008007171

10 9 8 7 6 5 4 3 2 1   9 10 11 12 13/0

Printed in Singapore   46
Reinforced Binding for Library Use
First printing, July 2007

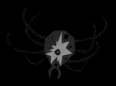

For everyone who added a thought or a word to
this book; for Grace, in whose office the monster was
born; and for Adrian, who made us dance and sing.

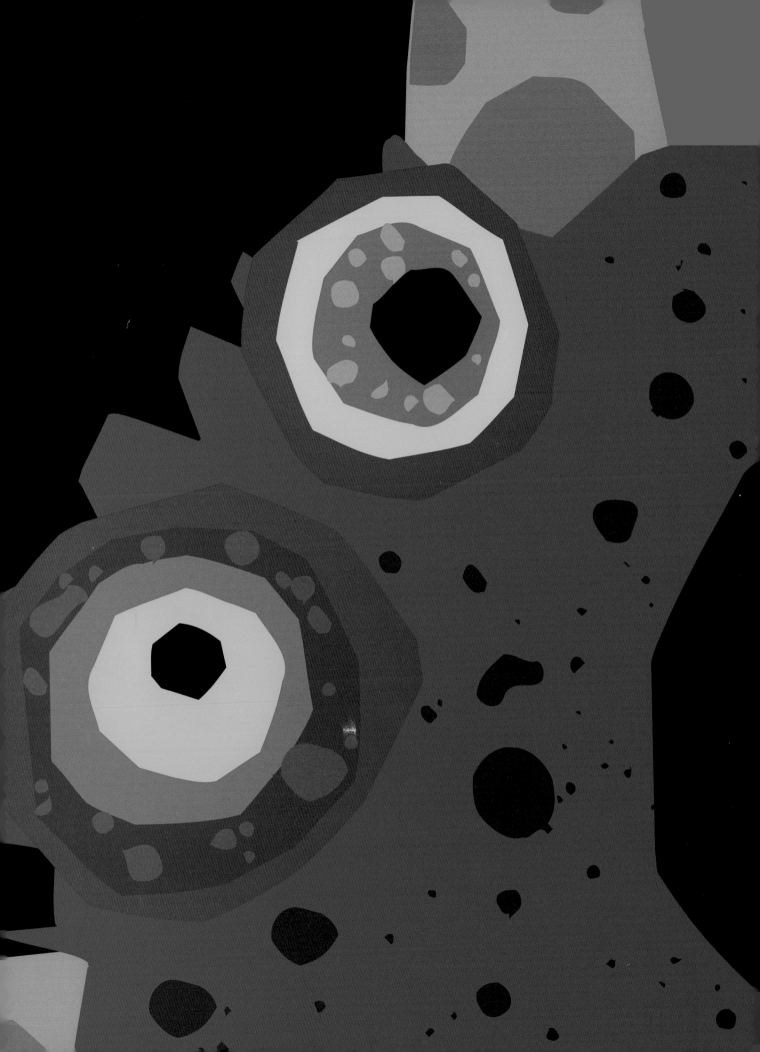

There was an old monster
who swallowed a tick.
I don't know why
he swallowed the tick
'cause it made him feel sick.

Next that old monster
he swallowed some ants.
He took a big chance
when he swallowed those ants

'cause man those ants
had him dancing in his pants.

Scritchy-
scratch,
Scritch,
scritchy-
scratch

Scritchy-
scratch,
Scritch,
scritchy-
scratch

He swallowed the ants
to catch the tick
but it didn't do the trick
'cause he STILL felt sick.

Then that old monster
he swallowed a lizard.
Yanked open his gizzard
and he swallowed that lizard.
He swallowed that lizard
to catch the ants

'cause man those ants
had him dancing in his pants.

scritchy-
scratch,
scritch,
scritchy-
scratch

He swallowed the ants
to catch the tick
but it didn't do the trick
'cause he STILL felt sick.

Next thing I know
he swallowed a bat.
Could you imagine that
when he swallowed that bat?

He swallowed the bat
to catch the lizard,
he swallowed the lizard
to catch the ants,
'cause man those ants
had him dancing in his pants.

scritchy-
scratch,
scritch,
scritchy-
scratch

Then he swallowed the ants
to catch the tick,
but it didn't do the trick
'cause he STILL felt sick.

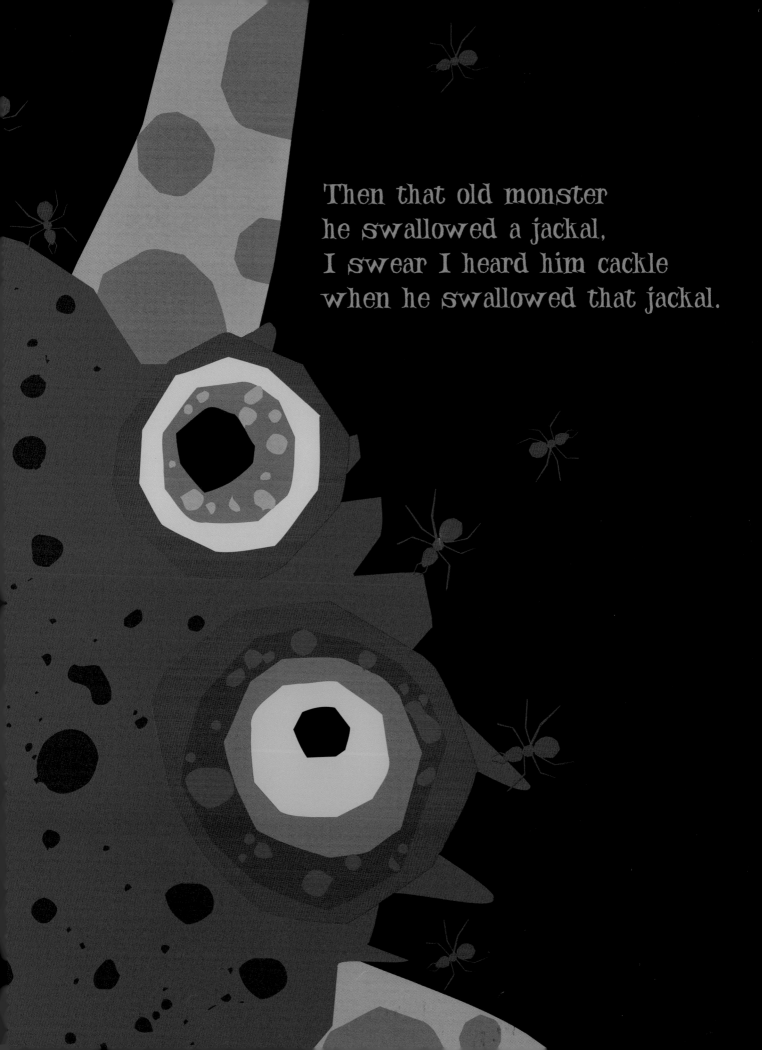

Then that old monster
he swallowed a jackal,
I swear I heard him cackle
when he swallowed that jackal.

He swallowed the jackal
to catch the bat,
he swallowed the bat
to catch the lizard,
he swallowed the lizard
to catch the ants,
'cause man those ants
had him dancing in his pants.

scritchy-
scratch,
scritch,
scritchy-
scratch

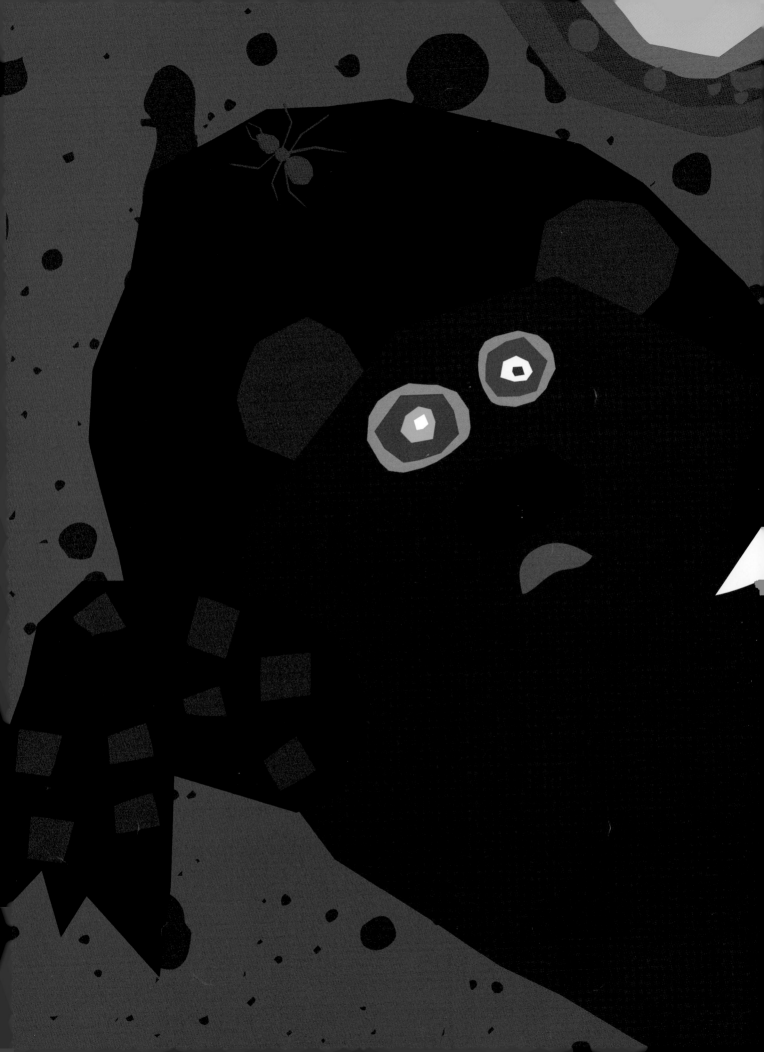

He swallowed the ants
to catch the tick
but it didn't do the trick
'cause he STILL felt sick.

Then he went and swallowed a bear,
you should have been there
when he swallowed that bear.

He swallowed the bear
to catch the jackal,
he swallowed the jackal
to catch the bat,
he swallowed the bat
to catch the lizard,
he swallowed the lizard
to catch the ants
'cause man those ants
were still making him dance.

scritchy-
scratch,
scritch,
scritchy-
scratch

He swallowed the ants
to catch the tick
but it didn't do the trick
'cause he STILL felt sick.

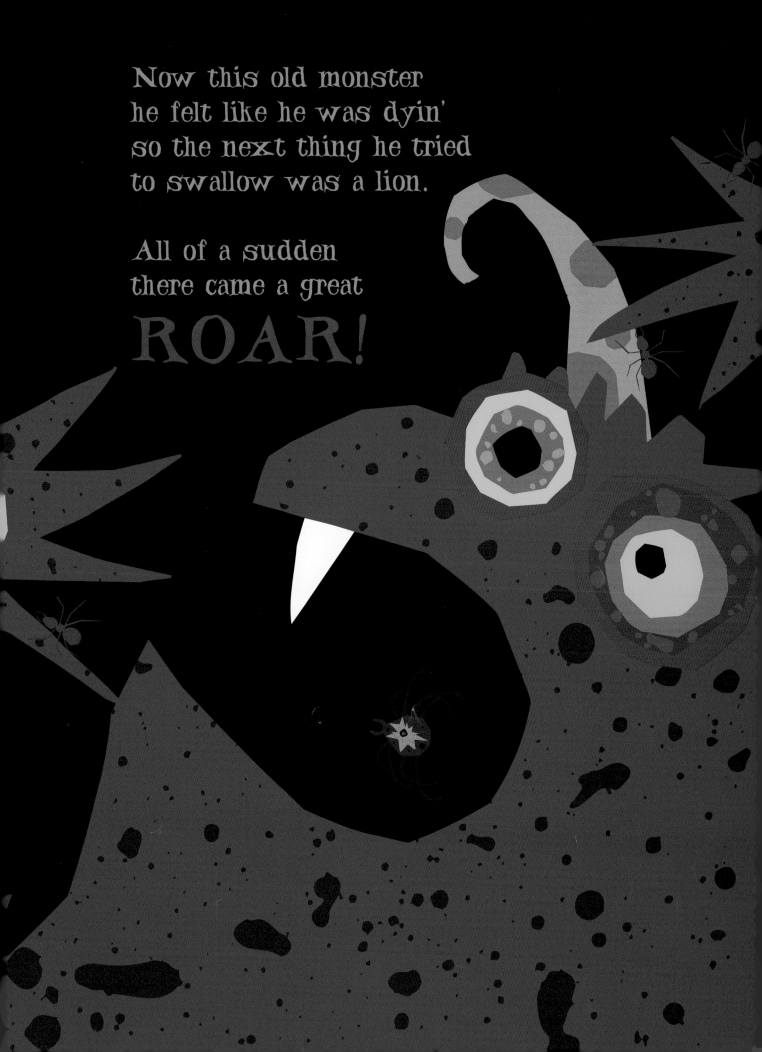

Now this old monster
he felt like he was dyin'
so the next thing he tried
to swallow was a lion.

All of a sudden
there came a great
ROAR!

And
that
monster
was
no
more!

scritchy-
   scratch,
scritch,
  scritchy-
    scratch

      scritchy-
        scratch,
      scritch,
      scritchy-
        scratch . . .